This book is dedicated to

MOCHA

2013, a year that forever changed our lives. I don't know where I would be with out you, and who knows where you would be with out me. I'm forever grateful for your friendship, your strengh, support and your guidance. You've taught me a lot, and I hope I've taught you just as much.
I've always said since day 1 "Who Rescued Who?"
Well, YOU rescued me and I'm honored to have rescued you.
You're 'MY SUPERHERO'!!!
Thank You for everything.
I love you Mocha!!

THANK YOU

★ ★ ★ ★ ★ ★ ★ ★ ★

To all service dog organizations and dog trainers across America that provide trained service dogs to the brave men and women who defend our freedom. Thank you! You strive to ensure our heroes receive care and comfort by pairing them up with man's best friend. I appreciate your commitment and dedication to our veterans. I am extremely grateful for Operation Delta Dog who provided me with my service dog, Mocha.

Thank you for the work you do!

MOCHA, THE SUPERHERO SERVICE DOG

WRITTEN BY DONALD JARVIS

A CREATIVE & CAPTIVATING STORY BY JARVISCRIPT BOOKS

1 Me Mocha!

"Oh, such a cute dog," a woman said. "Are you hungry? Here have this snack" the woman continued and she put her snack on the ground in front of me.

"Yes. Thank you, kind human lady." I said, and I gobbled the snack away. I looked up to see if the kind lady would give me more but she had walked away already. I sighed sadly. That day was just like any other day for me. No food and no owner.

Hi, I'm Mocha. Right now, I'm not wandering the streets of the city looking for food or kind humans. That was a long time ago. I now have an owner called Donnie, and I'm his service dog. Pretty cool right! Donnie is super cool too. I think he's a superhero because we go on heroic missions sometimes. But he keeps it a secret.

So back to what happened before....I used to live on the streets. I was hungry all the time; I had no baths, no love, and most of the time no friends. It was tough. But now that my life changed, my story on how I got here is worth sharing.

I hope you are ready for this, just like I'm always ready for a treat. My story will be sad sometimes but don't worry. I'm happy in the end. Let's continue where we stopped...

When the kind human lady left, I had to find more food somewhere else. I was a Black Lab Mix. I was not so big and I was not so small. I was the right size. I lived on almost every street in the city and spent a lot of my time searching for food and somewhere comfy to sleep. I did not have many friends, but I was very friendly. Maybe too friendly sometimes.

I woke up really hungry that day and I could smell fresh snacks coming from a store nearby. I ran over there with my quick four legs. I think I forgot that no one would just give me a free snack. So I sat outside watching people eat until the kind lady gave me her snack. As I walked away searching and trying to pick up the smell of more food, I saw one of my few friends Chubby Bunny. "Oh, no!" I whispered to myself. Chubby Bunny was a bunny who lived in the park. He always came out to play, eat, and have fun adventures with me and his other friends.

Chubby Bunny was nice and smart, but he ate a lot. I knew that if Chubby Bunny searched for food with me, Chubby Bunny would eat everything.

"Hello, my good friend. I am so glad to see you Mocha. You look like you are hungry," Chubby Bunny said.

"No. I am not hungry Chubby Bunny." I said trying to look innocent.

"Are you sure? I think I saw you sniffing for food?" Chubby Bunny said as he stood closer to me. Chubby Bunny also thought he could read minds.

I sighed again. "Okay. Okay. I have not found anything yet!" I said and I coughed. I had been coughing many times these past few days and I did not know why.

"Okay. Let's search together it will be an adventure!" Chubby Bunny said happily and he hopped along with me.

I coughed again and kept sniffing. We walked and walked through the city. Searching for food can be very hard in a big city. So we kept searching and sniffing and hopping. Soon we saw another friend called Willy Pigeon who lived on the tree by a small river.

"What's going on? Are you guys doing something fun without me," Willy Pigeon asked

"No, Willy Pigeon, we are just searching for food," I explained. "Okay, I'm in," he said.

He came out and went with us too. I was happy Willy Pigeon joined us. He could fly and his big funny-looking pigeon eyes could see food far away. He also liked to share, unlike Chubby Bunny.

"Can you see anything Willy Pigeon?" I asked.

"Nothing yet Mocha!" Screamed Willy Pigeon who was flying above us. "I can see a farm." He said after a while.

"A farm! I don't want to go to a farm. Those animals are mean!" Chubby Bunny said

"No, they are not," I said

"Yes, they are! The last time I went to a farm, the chickens chased me around. They were not friendly, " Chubby Bunny said.

"They were angry you ate all their food, and you did not want to share." Willy Pigeon screamed. Chubby Bunny just huffed and puffed. Willy Pigeon was right. I hoped Chubby Bunny would try to get along with the farm animals this time. We walked into the farm and the other animals there were quite friendly. We met a Pig called Pinky and some chickens. We even met a grumpy horse.

"Are you guys on an adventure?" Pinky the pig asked. She looked a little sad.

"No. We are actually just looking for food." I answered.

"Oh, come eat mine. I have a whole basket of fruits." Pinky said and before she could finish, Chubby Bunny was already grabbing some fruits.

I nodded my head as I looked at Chubby Bunny. "Thank you Pinky. Don't you have an owner?" I asked. I noticed the animal farm was really quiet and the animals looked like they lived alone. I knew that animals on a farm had an owner.

"Yes. But he has not come out of the house for a few days. I wonder if he's okay. We have food and everything we need on the farm," Pinky explained.

"Then why do you look so sad?" I asked Pinky

"I think my owner kept my blanket in the house and I am scared and cold without it at night" Pinky explained. She really looked sad and worried. I felt bad for her and wanted to help. At least to thank her for sharing her food.

"Hmmm..." I said. "Don't worry Pinky, maybe I can help". I ate some fruit and walked around the farm again. Animal farms sometimes had a leader. Sometimes it was a big dog, but I did not see a big dog on this farm. So, I went to speak to the grumpy horse.

"Hey," I said, but the horse turned away from me. I had to go around the horse.

"Hey... I just want to ask a question," I said.

"I don't want to know your question. I am trying to practice for my race." The horse said

"You have a race?" Chubby Bunny said suddenly. He appeared from nowhere and almost scared the horse. He had many apples in his hands and kept eating them one red apple at a time.

"Yes, I have a race. My owner will take me to race with other horses. I am going to be the fastest and strongest horse there." The horse said proudly smiling now.

"Wow. When is the race?" Chubby Bunny asked

"I don't know. My owner knows." The horse answered.

"Are you not worried about your owner? Pinky said he has not come out of the house for days." I said.

"You are right. So what should I do black dog?" the horse said. He was worried now.

"We need to get inside," I said with a serious face.

"Uh oh. It's hero time!" Willy Pigeon said as he flew towards us. Willy Pigeon liked stuff like this.

Chubby Bunny threw away all his apples, "Yayyy" he clapped. "So let's plan," he said.

Chubby Bunny found a stick and drew something on the ground.

"What's that?" I and the others asked

"A house," Chubby Bunny said. The drawing on the sand did not look like a house. "Isn't that a pineapple Chubby Bunny?" the horse asked

"It is? Well, it's a pineapple house," Chubby Bunny said.

"But our owner's house is not a pineapple," the horse said.

"We don't have to draw the house for our plan," I said, and I coughed again.

"You have been coughing a lot Mocha, did you eat something bad?" Chubby Bunny asked me.

"I don't know," I said sadly, "Come on, let's find a way into the house,"

So I, Chubby Bunny, Willy Pigeon, and the horse came out of the farm and went towards the house. We looked for the door or somewhere to get in. Willy Pigeon found the door, but it was locked. There was a hole in the door.

"Who can fit into the hole?" the horse asked.

"Willy Pigeon can," I said.

"What? Why me! The house looks dark inside. I don't like dark places. I am not going in there." Willy Pigeon screamed.

"How about you Chubby Bunny?" the horse asked.

"You are not such a big horse. You can try. Or Mocha can try. Willy Pigeon is right, the house looks dark and I don't like dark," Chubby Bunny said

"So who is going to go in?" the horse cried.

As they argued I saw an open window and while the others talked about who could go in, I ran to the window and jumped inside. The house was dark because the lights were off. I opened the front door for the others. I had to scratch the handle a few times.

"Oh, how did you get in Mocha? You are so brave, " Willy Pigeon said. We went around the house but did not find the owner. The house was clean and quiet. I tried to sniff around for Pinky's blanket. I found the smell. It was coming from a basket in the room. I pulled the basket to the ground and searched the clothes for the blanket. I found it.

"Yes!" I said. "There is no one here. Do you think your owner is missing?" Willy Pigeon asked the horse.

"Hmm..." Mocha said, "This is a mystery."

"Your owner has disappeared or abandoned you like some people abandon animals," Chubby Bunny said suddenly looking sad.

"Really? Oh, no... what about my race," the horse said confused.

"Aha!" I shouted. I saw a ticket

"I think he went on a vacation..." Chubby Bunny said looking at the ticket. "What? Who would take care of us now?" the horse screamed. "Maybe he will come back soon," I told the horse, and they all agreed with me.

We went out of the house and tried to lock the door. I gave Pinky her blanket and she squealed with joy. She even told us to take more apples. I was just happy to help. I think that is why I get along with my current owner, Donnie. He likes helping people too.

We said goodbye to the others at the farm, and walked back into the city. Chubby Bunny went to the park and Willy Pigeon went to the tree beside the lake. That day was a good day.

2 Somewhere new!

After my adventure with Chubby Bunny and Willy Pigeon, I did not see them for the next few days. I kept wandering new streets in the city until I wandered into the backyard of a house. I sniffed something nice and sweet and went to check what it was. Suddenly, the lights came on and someone saw me.

"Look, Peter, it's a dog outside our house" a woman screamed. She did not look friendly and neither did the angry man that came outside. He had a big stick and he called me a bad dog. I was not a bad dog, I just thought I smelled food. He also called me an ugly and dirty dog. It hurt me but I could not stay there and cry. I had to run because the angry man chased me with his stick.

"Come here, you stupid dog!" he screamed and the woman even said, "Get him, Peter!"
I ran as fast as I could out of the yard but the man kept chasing me. He got close once and hit me with the stick but I just kept running. Soon he stopped chasing me, but I never noticed. I ran and ran until I ran into a dark empty street. I did not see the angry man coming, so I hid under an empty carton nearby.

I was tired from all the running. I was hungry, cold, and sad. I slept off. When I opened my eyes, the next morning, there was a bird looking at me.

"Who are you?" the bird asked.

"I'm Mocha. Who are you?" I asked too.

"A bird, as you can see. Why are you here?" the bird asked again.

"Oh, no." This bird reminded me of Willy Pigeon. Pigeons ask a lot of questions and never answer correctly when you ask them back.

I knew this bird won't leave me alone if I just stayed there. I tried to get up. I was so tired and my body hurt. I looked around, but I did not know where I was. I wanted to ask someone for directions. The bird was still there staring at me. I sighed.

"Where am I?" I asked. I hoped he would know.

"Oh, you mean the name of this place?" the bird asked.

"Yes," I said smiling, I thought he understood.

"Oh yes. Well, this place is emmm.... Well, I don't know do I look like I know. I don't!" the bird said.

I sat back down, confused. I knew I was lost. I got lost running from the angry man. I did not know where I was.

I coughed and coughed and coughed.

I decided to rest a little. I closed my eyes and slept off again. Many days passed by like this. I was always tired, hungry, and coughing.

After a long time, something else happened. "Oh, this poor doggy," a voice said.

I opened my tired eyes and saw two men standing in front of me.

"Come on buddy, let's take you somewhere safe," the other man said and they picked me up and put me in a van.

I saw other dogs in the van too. Many of them looked hungry and tired too.

"You look worse than all of us. I'm Luna What's your name?" a white dog asked

"Mocha," I said tired. I knew I looked terrible. I even felt worse.

"Where are we going?" I asked.

"I heard it's called a Shelter. It's a place where they keep animals like us who live alone on the streets." Luna said

"I don't care where I go as long as there's food and a house," another dog said. He was the biggest but had such a small voice.

I hoped they were right. I slept off again.

I woke up when someone carried me again. They took us to a place where there were many animals in different cages. They seemed okay. The kind humans put me in a cage too and they gave me food and water. I was too tired to eat, but I tried.

"I think this one needs to see a vet," one woman said.

"Yes, me too. He seems very sick," a man said.

"But if he is so sick, we would have to put him down." The woman continued. Some other animals gasped.

"That's sad. Okay. Let us watch him for some days," the man said.

I did not know what they were talking about but the other animals seemed to know. "Hey. What do they mean put down?" I asked the cat in the cage by my side

"It's when you close your eyes and never open them again. You will be buried and forgotten." The cat said with a serious face.

"What? I am still confused" I did not know what they were talking about.

"She means you are going to die black dog. You are sick. No one will take a sick dog," another dog said.

I understood now. I looked at myself in the bowl of water. I was sad. I closed my eyes and imagined I had a happy home with a human I could lick and lots of food. I even imagined I had a bath and I was fresh and clean.

I whimpered.

Some days passed and I did not get better. I made new friends in the shelter, even though I was always too tired to talk to them.

The cat beside me was Lily. She was black and thought she was ugly. I thought she was wrong, but she never believed me. The big dog was Bailey. He was like a leader. I liked him too.

One day, some new humans came. Some came with little children. I loved kids. They were always nice. They looked at all of us and picked the animal they liked.

"They are adopting us. I hope someone would take me," Lily screamed. I could hear a few animals talking. "Pick me! Pick me!" some shouted "I'm over here. I'm a good pet, pick me too!" others shouted.

I could not shout like them so I just sat there.

"Mom, look at this one. I like him" one boy said. He tried to rub behind my ears and I tried to lick his face. He smelled nice. I wondered if he would take me home with him.

"Oh sweetie you can't take him. He's sick. Take another doggy" they said to the boy. He looked at me and I saw he felt bad.

"Bye doggy" he said and even though he could not hear me, I said goodbye too. The boy picked Bailey.

"I will miss you all my friends" Bailey barked as he was taken.

"Bye Bailey," I and the others said.

Many animals were picked too and finally later that day, a little girl came with her father.

She wanted Lily. "Someone wants me?" Lily asked surprised

"I told you. You are not ugly. Good luck Lily" I said weakly

"You will be fine Mocha. Goodbye" Lily said and she was taken from her cage.

I closed my eyes again and when I opened them, a woman was staring at me.

"I can take him. I'm a dog trainer. Let me take him" She said to one of the people at the shelter.

"Alright," they told her and the kind dog trainer lady took me away.

3 Superhero Service Dog

We went to a place called 'the vet'. I saw a few animals with their owners waiting to enter a room. There was a hamster who kept saying he did not want to enter the room. He cried about it for hours.

"Why are you making so much noise?!" a cat screamed at him.

"Don't you know? This is the vet's place. He will poke you with needles and wear you plastic. It is horrible! Horrible I say!" the hamster said dramatically. He succeeded in scaring a puppy.

"You mean it's bad?" the puppy said and he started to bother his owner. He barked and whimpered. He did not want to go into the room anymore. But after spending some hours at the vet, I learned that you might not have a choice. I also learned that the vet makes you feel better.

The vet told the dog trainer lady that I was very sick with heartworms and they would need lots of money and time to treat me. I thought I would be abandoned again. But the dog trainer lady did not abandon me.

The heartworms made me sick all this time. The vet said there were long hungry worms in my body. They were making me very, very sick.

I took a lot of medications. I did not do much exercising. I ate. I was no longer cold or hungry. I was happy.

After a long time, I felt fine. The dog trainer lady was happy and she took me somewhere new. I met other dogs there and made new friends.

"Hey, I'm Mocha. What are we doing here?" I asked a big brown dog.

"We are training to be superheroes, my friend." He said. "I'm Dud. I have been training for a long time. Soon my work in the world will begin." Dud said. He made me think of the police dogs I saw sometimes.

I wondered how we could train to be superheroes.

"Don't think too much about it Mocha. We are going to be superheroes with our own humans. You will see. Someone will come for you." Another dog called Deb said.

"No one has ever come for me. Only the kind dog trainer lady who saved me." I said. "You will see Mocha. Come on let's play" Deb said and we played fetch with the trainers. They had plenty of balls to throw.

I saw what Deb meant before when a human came to meet her. Deb went with the human sometimes and her training to become a superhero service dog started.

I was happy for her.

One day, a human named Donnie came to see me. I liked his smell. It was nice and kind and somehow sad. I wondered why he was sad.

"His name is Mocha. He is a strong dog. He's suffered a lot before." The dog trainer lady said to Donnie.

"Hi, Mocha. I'm Donnie. I hope we can be friends." Donnie said.

I looked at him and barked. I licked his face. "Of course we can be friends," I said.

"Oh, I think he likes you," the dog trainer lady said.

"Really? Okay, let's begin I guess." Donnie said and he took me with him.

"I'm going to be a superhero!" I shouted to Dud as I left with Donnie.

"Good thing kid. We will save the world!" Dud said. He really really made me think of police dogs. Those dogs were so serious.

I started seeing Donnie many times in a week. The dog trainer was teaching both of us hero stuff. I thought dog trainers only trained dogs.

I thought Donnie would have to keep visiting me every day. After a few weeks, Donnie took me home.

"Welcome home Mocha," Donnie said when we got into his house.

It was a great house. "These are some pictures from when I was in the army. I got injured and sent home Mocha, that's why I need you. Many veterans like me need buddies like you." Donnie said as he rubbed my head. I liked when he rubbed me.

We went to the see the dog trainer every week. I learned many things about being a superhero service dog and about Donnie too.

Donnie did not know dog language, but I was happy to teach him. I learned more human language too.

Sometimes Donnie would say, "Come Mocha. Come."

I would just stare at him. Then he would hold a treat and I remembered the meaning of the word, "Come."

Sometimes, I wanted a belly rub. But Donnie would rub behind my ears. I had to lie down on my back for him to understand.

"Don't worry Donnie. You will learn dog language soon" I said. I made sure I taught him every day, even when the dog trainer was not there. He taught me too and I loved it when he used treats to help me remember. Woof! Treats are delicious.

I noticed that Donnie was sad and worried sometimes, especially when there were too many people around.

I learned to sit between him and people. I always told them, "Stay away from my human" Even though they could not hear me, I'm sure they understood.

At night I learned to wake Donnie up if he was having a bad dream. I would lick his face and poke him until he stopped.

The classes were always fun. Woof! I was a happy dog.

One day, something scary happened. Donnie took me on a thing called an elevator. I knew the elevator was not my friend. But Donnie did not understand. I think he thought my scared bark was my happy bark. I whimpered throughout the time I was in the elevator. I made sure Donnie knew I did not like it. When we left, I also made sure I barked a little at the elevator for scaring me and many people.

After a fun year training to be a superhero, I graduated! Donnie and I were very proud. Dud was proud of me too.

"I knew you could do it friend" Dud said.

"I will miss you Dud" I told him

"Me too, Mocha. Make all the superhero dogs proud, " Dud said.

"Are you crying Dud?" I asked, surprised to see a shiny tear in Dud's eye.

"No! Superheroes don't cry. I am...just...." Dud tried to explain looking confused. "I understand Dud. I cry too. Thank you for being my friend," I said.

Donnie and I brought a gift to my graduation. It was a letter from the President of the United States. The President was a nice man and in the letter he thanked our dog training school for rescuing dogs like me and giving the dogs to veterans who were happy to have them. The President sent his picture too.

I wanted to thank the dog trainers too. So, I licked all their faces before we left. They liked it.

I continued to go everywhere with Donnie. Sometimes he took me to meet other people called veterans. They were in the army too. I always notice that they are like Donnie was when we met before. They were sad and lonely. I licked their faces. I sat on their legs. I barked and smiled at them. They were happy. I loved my superhero work.

As a service dog, I wear a uniform. All superheroes have uniforms too. When I am in public, people can't pet me or give me treats. It's distracting for a service dog. I am serious about my superhero job. I must support Donnie. There are a lot of people like Donnie who need the help of service dogs like me. Many of them are veterans who worked in the army but could not make any friends or be happy when they came home. Sometimes they are sick and alone like I was. Dogs like me, Dud and Deb help them be happy and strong.

It was fun and I loved Donnie. We traveled on airplanes and I saw the clouds very close to us. We even watch baseball and basketball together. I saw lots of humans watching too and shouting when the ball went into a net. It was strange but I liked it because Donnie liked it.

So, this is where my story ends. I live with Donnie now and I am happy. I wish I could tell all the dogs and humans never to give up in their lives. If I could have a happy life now, after being sick, hungry, and cold on the streets, then anything good can happen for anyone. I have to go wake Donnie, today is soccer day. He loves watching soccer.

Goodbye from Mocha the Superhero Service Dog.
And Donnie too, his superhero service human.
Woof!

September 5, 2014

I send greetings as you gather in support of veterans in your community.

In America, we take responsibility for ourselves and each other, for the ideals we embrace and the future we share. We celebrate selflessness, and we value those who take steps to make a difference in the lives of others.

Your organization embodies this proud tradition in Massachusetts. By lifting up our veterans and connecting them to man's best friend, you not only strive to ensure our heroes receive care and comfort, you also help animals in need find loving homes. These efforts reflect the spirit of a grateful Nation and remind us that we are strongest together.

I am deeply grateful to our veterans and their loved ones for their extraordinary sacrifices, and I appreciate all those who give back to the men and women who defended our freedom. I wish you the very best as you continue this important work in the years ahead.

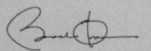

Made in the USA
Middletown, DE
04 January 2020